One Way

Short Stories About Left Turns

By Dorsey Howard, Jr.

Heart Thoughts Publishing
Floyds Knobs, IN

Printed in the United States of America

First Printing, 2013

ISBN-13: 978-1490495620
ISBN-10: 1490495622
LCCN: 2013943499

Heart Thoughts Publishing
P. O. Box 536
Floyds Knobs, IN 47119

Dedication

I would like to dedicate this book to my mom, Barbara, for not giving up on her son when he had given up on himself. To my dad whom I know did the best he knew how. To my stepfather and uncle for giving me the knowledge and skills to survive the gangs, tough streets, and projects of Chicago. To my sisters and brothers who had to live with the terror I brought home. To my kids and grandbabies who have been there for me, no matter what. To every family that has lost a loved one. I give big thanks to my God, that one person who never ever let me down. He taught me to know that I'm blessed, even on the worst days. When I didn't believe in Him, He believed in me. He put it in my heart to want to save a kid's life. I pray that this will help save many lives.

Table of Contents

Introduction

LEFT TURNS

What are left turns?

I believe that we make left turns anytime we do something wrong. This can be anything from a curse word, a lie, murder, and everything in between. Everyone has made left turns in life. Most people started making left turns when they were children. Left turns can be as addictive as drugs, sex, or alcohol. These turns can lead to a terrible life. In time, they will lead you straight to jail or prison, if you're lucky. At worst, left turns will lead you to the graveyard, (death).

Most my life I blamed my mom for leaving me as a kid. I blamed my dad for beating my mom and me. I blamed my sister for always lying about me. I blamed both parents for divorcing and moving me from a nice big house to the projects of Chicago. Over time, I realized that we all have excuses or reasons for making left turns.

What's your reason for making left turns? **Who do you blame?**

My goal is to have kids and teens take a look at their lives and try to stop making left turns. All I'm asking is for you to try practicing right turns, before it's too late.

I'm a survivor from a life of left turns. When faced with the next left turn in your life, and there will be left turns, TRY RIGHT. If I survived and was able to turn my life around, YOU CAN TOO!!

Warning: If you continue making left turns, you will have a rough life ahead, if your next left doesn't kill you.

My God allowed me to make it to this point in life to share this with you. If nothing else, just give it a try. You may just love living right. I do. The life you save may be your own.

I recently had a conversation with my childhood friend, Lawrence Perkins, who is now an educator and an author. We both grew up in the same housing projects in Chicago. He asked me what had happened that finally made me want to change my life? I was stuck with so much to say. As I pondered his question, I had so many thoughts flashing in my head. Where to begin? It was like I had so many answers for him, I didn't know where to start. I thought I was losing my mind.

I remembered the time when I was in jail and got into it with the guards. They came in to get me, and I started fighting with them. They ended up beating me so badly that my court date had to be changed. I was put into solitary confinement with no clothes. I sat there and cried so hard. I asked God, "Why me? Why was my life so messed up?" I thought of how tired I was of facing death, over and over again. I lived a hard life in the projects and was almost sexually assaulted as a runaway kid on the west side of Chicago. I was tired of beating on the women in my life that I may have loved, tired of being beaten by police, tired of having guns in my face. I thought about so many reasons why I didn't want this life anymore. I had been a crack head, then I turned into a meth addict. I was tired of being a drunk. I was tired of being a member of a gang. I was tired of going in and out of jail and prisons. I was tired of not being there for my kids. I thought about how I tried to take my own life but was saved, shortly before death, by my own child. All because I couldn't stop making left turns. I always wanted to change, but there wasn't any hope for a bad kid coming from the projects, with no education and knowing nothing about life, but left turns. I couldn't take it anymore.

I remembered sitting in the courtroom once, thinking that it would be the same as usual. I would either get released, go to treatment, or be sent back to prison for a year or so. As I sat in the courtroom, the prosecutor asked if he could approach the bench. They whispered to each other and pulled out some big books. As they started flipping through pages, I started to get nervous. I looked back at my mom, who was the only one in the courtroom. I shook my head thinking they were doing something illegal. I had never been in a courtroom where I was the only case. I knew something was wrong. I felt it in my gut. I also knew that the most I could get for the crime was 48 months.

The prosecutor and my public defender came back to the table. My public defender wasn't looking happy at all. I tried to whisper and ask him what was going on. Before I could finish asking him, the prosecutor stated that they considered me to be a career criminal. This really scared me. The reason for my fear was that I knew I could get 25 years to life in prison. All the breath from my body was gone, I felt like I was about to die. I prayed to God, "Lord, don't let them do this to me. Please Father please." My attorney objected and the big book came out again. This time, my public defender asked to approach the bench. They talked and then came back to the table. I looked back at my mom with hurt, anger, shame and blame. We both looked confused and worried.

I ended up getting only two years. From that moment on I started praying, begging God for forgiveness. I prayed for change. I knew that they hadn't called me a career criminal and given me twenty five years to life in prison this time. But I also knew that I had been going to jail at least once a year, and the next time I came into their court room for anything, they were going to give it to me. I knew I'd never see freedom again. I could feel my life changing as I was doing my time in prison.

On my way out of prison, for the first time in my life, I gave up on trying to live my way. I was afraid that if I got back into trouble, I may be gone for life. Weeks before my release I started thinking about how my God has never let me down. I thought about how He had never lied once to me, so I started asking Him to lead my life. I vowed to follow. I prayed that same prayer as I walked out the prison doors. I was scared and very nervous, thinking about that prosecutor calling me a career criminal.

I got out feeling like a new person. I held my head high. I soon realized that I was living free of everything and of everyone. I stopped going around people that were doing wrong. I got my GED and went to college. I started going to church and started trying to live a different life. For the first time in my life, I was taking rights. I was living right, and started loving life. For the first time in my life I felt free.

Today I feel like a new man. My whole life has changed from a life full of left turns, to taking rights, and living a wonderful life.

If I can do it, SO CAN YOU.

A Life of Lefts, Turned Right

This was me when my life was full of left turns. I was one of the lucky ones to have gotten caught and sent to prison. If I had not been sent to prison, I would be dead today, either from the drugs and alcohol or from someone killing me.

My attitude about life changed for the better while in prison. I realized that I hated myself and the life I was living. I stopped making left turns and started getting to know more about my higher power, which is God. I begged and pleaded with Him to not let me go right back to that life of lefts. I knew from the past that I didn't want to live like that anymore but was powerless and couldn't change my life on my own. I could tell, while I was still in prison, that my life was changing for the better. But I knew that the real test would be when I got back on the streets. I was released in 2008 and never looked back. God made changes in my life that I never thought was possible.

It doesn't matter where you're at in life, where you live, or how bad you think your life is. Know that you can make it. When faced with your next left turn, please turn right, or at least try. I've seen so many people take left turns, not knowing it would be the last turn they will ever take in life. Don't let this happen to you.

As a kid coming up in the projects, it seemed like everyone and everything around me was about left turns. Nothing was right. One thing for sure, I made it, and no matter what your life looks like, you can too. Don't get me wrong, I'm not the only one who made it.

You will never know if the next left turn you take will be your last, so why take that chance? A good place to start, before you get to that turn, is to plan to go right. School, a job, church and God or your higher power is a good place to begin. It took me almost forty years to get it. I got lucky/blessed to have made it. You may not be so lucky. I'm trying to give it to you, the best way I know how, because if you get it while you are young, the sky is your limit. There is nothing in this world you can't achieve when you're trying to live life right. You only have one life to live, so start living it right.

Here's a few of my stories. I would like for you to put yourself into these stories, and tell me what you think went wrong. Who made the left turns and why? Would you have done anything differently? I hope and pray that you get the point and pass it on. Maybe you can help save a child's life. All I need from you is to just say no to left turns in life and try right. Consider these right turns:

- No matter what, respect your mother and father.
- Stop lying.
- Walk away from drugs and alcohol.
- Don't steal.
- Stand on your own two feet and walk away from gangs.
- Put down the guns. Don't shoot it out, talk it out.
- Don't take another's life. Live and let live. Walk away.
- Finish school, get your GED, do some volunteer work or go to college.
- Take care of your kids.
- Try church. It's plain and simple.

You can do it.

Stop now, chose life over death, before it's too late. If I can do it, you can too.

Chapter 1 – **Stop the Car**

BOOM, BOOM, BOOM, BOOM, BOOM, BOOM, BOOM was the horrible sounds of gun shots going off. I froze for a minute, which seemed like forever, and just prayed in my mind , "God please, please, don't let it be."

It was a perfect eighty-five degree day. The sun was nice and bright, and the sky was clear and blue. There was very little wind blowing, a perfect day to be on the lake, in a boat, or something. We all wanted to do something for Tony's birthday, so we decided to have a barbeque. As usual, with the barbeque came drinking and smoking.

A song from Tupac came on that I loved called, "Me Against The World." I went to where the music was and turned it all the way up. The sound of the bass had the walls jumping. Some girl, who was there with Tony's girl, said "Hey", and started dancing. This started a flow of everyone dancing around the yard, some of the women had on high heels that were getting stuck in the dirt. Everyone was smiling, clapping, and having the time of their lives.

It always made me happy when I could get people together just having fun. I would go broke at times. If you smoked, you were high. If you drank, you were drunk. People ate until they were full, and the vibe was always comfortable and very relaxing. People that couldn't dance were doing whatever they wanted to call it. It was fun, but funny. Yes, this was one of the best days ever.

I was wondering what was happening outside. I heard everyone, all excited, as they were saying hello to one of our family members, who was about to become a pro basketball player. I looked out the window to see that it was Mike. He didn't come around the family much, but when he did we always made the best of it.

Mike and his new wife had just given birth to a baby boy. They were the couple everyone wanted to be. Mike's brother, Ant, was with them. Ant was the total opposite of Mike. Ant was a true thug who was an active member of a Chicago gang. He had recently been released from prison and was possibly on his way back if he continued making left turns.

Ant wanted to go get some more liquor and asked who wanted to ride with him. Ant was fun to be around and told jokes about everyone, so people loved being around him. Mike and I decided we wanted to ride with Ant. Mike's wife wanted to go also, and she got mad because Mike wouldn't let her come with us. She started saying things like, "Why I can't ever have any fun? I'm always stuck with the baby." Mike gave in. His wife won that fight. So off we went driving to the liquor store.

We all sat in the car while Ant went in and got the drinks. When he came out of the store, two guys, dressed in red, started beating him. When we jumped out to help, they took off running. Ant was mad and couldn't let it go. He got into the car and started driving fast and crazy, talking about how he was going to kill them.

As we passed our turn to the house, I said, "Where are you going?" He didn't answer.

As we turned onto the street where I knew the opposite gang lived, I knew Ant was about to start trouble. I told him to stop the car, but he didn't. I grabbed the wheel and told him to not make that left turn. He pulled over and said in a very loud voice, "Get out of my car little punk."

I looked at Mike and his wife and told them to get out with me, but they refused. I told them that Ant was taking them into a neighborhood that he was not welcomed in. I could see in Mike's wife's eyes that she was scared and wanted to get out the car, but Mike was all excited and wanted to go see what happened. Mike had never experienced this kind of life and was very excited to ride along. Ant had told me, in no uncertain terms, to get out of the car. Before I could get both feet out the car, he drove off, peeling out very fast. His tires were smoking as he fishtailed his car down the street. I hollered at him, **"Please, don't make that left turn!"**

As I started walking back to my house, I watched the car turn left onto a block which I knew was a dead end street. I didn't think Ant knew that this street had only one way in and one way out. For some stupid reason, he turned onto it.

Two or three minutes later I heard a bang. It sounded like a gunshot, but I wasn't sure. I froze. It was like I was paralyzed as I heard the shots from semiautomatic weapons going off like it was a war zone. I found myself running towards the block where Ant turned left, but something snapped me out of it. I froze again and turned around. I ran home screaming, "No! Please God, please, don't let it be." The tears rolled down my face.

I stopped half a block from my house and wiped the tears from my eyes. I thought, "What if they are back? Ant already thinks of me as a punk." I didn't want him to see me crying. I was calm for a moment, but before I could reach my house, I heard sirens, lots of them. Police, ambulances, and fire trucks were speeding down the street. I began praying out loud again, now begging my God, "Please, please don't let it be."

When I walked in the door, my mom was sitting there rocking Mike and his wife's new baby to sleep. I thought I would play it off like nothing was wrong, but as soon as my mother saw me, she knew. She asked what was wrong and where everyone else was. I couldn't hold back any longer, and I burst out in tears. I started crying like a baby. I told her I didn't know. But I felt it in my heart that the shooting had something to do with them not being here. I didn't want to say anything and make everyone panic.

Out of the blue came a loud, scary scream from the other room. It was my sister, who was watching T. V., and the news of a deadly shooting interrupted her show. We all ran to the T. V. They didn't have any information yet but said that there were two confirmed dead at the scene, a male and female. The house went into a crazy depression when they showed pictures of

Ant's car with lots of bullet holes in it. It looked like they were in a war zone in another country. People started screaming and hollering. Everyone had tears in their eyes. My mom hollered, "Why him? Why wasn't it you?" I ran with hurt and never stopped running.

Ant was paralyzed, and would be in a wheelchair for the rest of his life. Mike and his new wife were killed instantly, all because Ant wouldn't GO RIGHT.

Chapter 2 - **Kids, Drugs, and Alcohol**

"Man, I stole a couple cigarettes from my aunt last night; I took a puff and choked. My head was spinning; I choked and felt like I was flying on cloud nine. I still had one left," Dee said to Willie as he proudly showed him the cigarette.

We had to have been only ten or eleven years old. Everyone thought Dee was a good kid who would grow up to do something special with his life. Dee was a smart kid and got good grades in school. As Dee lit the Newport, he began to choke again. "Wow I'm high," he said as tears rolled down his face. His eyes were blood shot red.

Willie was a cool kid whose mom and dad had great jobs and dressed him very well. Willie started choking and passed it to Eddie. After a few times of smoking cigarettes, they weren't getting that high anymore.

Eddie's mom sold weed. One day Eddie and Willie came to my house all excited to show me something. They showed me the weed, and I said, "Let's get high." I stole a couple tall cans of Budweiser beer from my dad. We ran to our little spot over by the basketball court.

Willie started singing, "We're going to get high, we're going to get high." I was thinking, yes, we are about to get messed up for the very first time.

We had a song we made up. We started singing,

"Higher, higher. We're moving on up, moving on up. Getting higher, higher, moving on up, we're moving on up. Smoking that bow, drinking that rose, snorting that coke, shooting that dope."

Today I sing that same song with a twist.

"STOP getting higher, higher, you're not moving on up, you're not moving on up. Stop smoking that bow, stop drinking that rose, stop snorting that coke, stop shooting that dope. You betta' stop, getting higher, higher; you're not moving on up. You'll find yourself stuck."

Over the next few years, we were drinking almost daily. We were drinking hard liquor. The weed wasn't working anymore, so we started snorting heroin and cocaine. We used to be best friends, but the drugs started turning us against each other. Crack cocaine came out, and Willie wanted to make money, so he started selling it. Willie never knew that Eddie was smoking crack and may have been an addict. Dee sold weed and became a young alcoholic.

One night, Eddie came to Dee's house acting all wired like he had been smoking crack all day. Dee was trying to tell Eddie to eat and sleep at his house that night, but crack takes away your hunger, so Eddie didn't want to eat or sleep. What he did ask Dee was if he would help him rob their best friend, Willie.

Eddie had this little 38 hand gun that he borrowed from his older brother without his brother's knowledge. I told him, "Man, that's one of our best friends, don't ever say anything like that to me again. If you go ask Willie, I'm sure he will give you what you want."

Just the thought of Eddie saying that made me mad and I told him to get out of my house. I said, "Man, go home and get some rest. I'll talk to you tomorrow." I told him to leave the gun just in case the police stopped him. But he refused to leave his brother's gun.

Eddie said, "You're right man, I'm going home."

***

Everyone in the house was awakened by someone acting like they were going to beat our door down. As I got up, I looked at the clock. It was 3:15 am. I heard my dad holler," Who is it?" My first thought was that it was Eddie and that I would be in big trouble for him coming to our house at this time of morning. When I peeked around to see who my dad was talking to, I saw that it was four police officers looking for Eddie. I got closer and heard my mom burst out screaming and crying. The officer stated that Eddie was wanted for the robbery and murder of Willie Thomas, our best friend.

Willie was dead and another best friend, Eddie, got life without parole for killing him.

Put the guns down. It's so much easier to shoot and kill someone when you've got that gun in your hand. There have been plenty of times I wished I had my gun.

But I soon realized that if I would have had it, I wouldn't be here writing these stories.

Just like that, left turns took both my friends away from me forever.

Chapter 3 - **Riding on Top of Elevator**

The Robert Taylor Homes were projects on the Southside of Chicago where Dee spent most of his childhood life. These were big, brick buildings, some were red and others were white. They had sixteen floors with ten apartments on each floor. They were kind of spooky at night when the elevators didn't work. You had to walk up the stairs. Most the time you would get so far up, and all of a sudden you would get to a spot where there would be total darkness because either the bulb blew or people just busted them out.

Dee was a tough little kid, but at times he would get a little frightened going up those dark hallways. The hallways had a strong odor of urine that was at times so strong you had to hold your breath. These projects seemed like prison buildings. There wasn't much for kids to do, so Dee and his buddies joined a gang. Dee loved being a part of something so big, he felt like he belonged. Little did they know, they were all taking a big left turn when they joined the gang.

They were young kids with nothing to do and nowhere to turn. So they all started drinking, smoking weed, and doing things like robbing the beer truck when it came around to make a delivery. Dee and his friends would jump into the back of semi-trucks when they would be sitting at a red light. They would open the back door and start throwing out as many boxes as they could until either the light changed or the driver would see them. They were bored little teens wanting something to do.

There were nice, hot summer days when people would be out playing softball, having a good time. Dee and his buddies loved playing softball so much that they joined a softball team called the Wrecking Crew. And yes, they wrecked almost every team they played. In the projects, they didn't play with gloves. You caught the ball with your bare hands. One year the Wrecking Crew was beating everyone in their league so badly that they had to play teams older and bigger. That year their team came in first place. They were given certificates and trophies for being the best. This was a moment Dee would never forget. But soon Dee and his friends were back taking left turns again.

Dee's friend, Chill, was an older guy. Chill was taller than everyone else. He was light-skinned or what we would call a "high yellow" brother who loved to sing. Chill had a piece of metal that the firemen used to help people off broken elevators. Chill was also the only one tall enough to reach the opening to get on top of the elevator. When Dee first saw Chill open an elevator with the metal, he stepped back very quickly. Dee stopped fast in his tracks, thinking to himself, "I can't show fear." But he was scared.

When Chill rolled that big door open, Dee felt like death was looking him in the face. All you could see was gloomy darkness. There were maybe five steel strings coming down the middle. The elevator was right there so you could just step onto the top. It was like looking into death's eyes: cold, dark and scary. Chill jumped right on and told Dee to come on. He explained where not to stand and how all the buttons worked. You controlled everything from the top.

The fear was gone very quickly. Dee was very excited and wanted to know more. They let the big door close. Chill pushed a button, and off they went.

Chill said, "We are going to pick up some people so be quiet." He pushed a button and they were on the first floor. They got excited as they watched people get onto this elevator. They knew that they had total control over these people's lives. The elevator went up a couple floors where they let this old lady get off. Chill said, "Now let's have some fun." He whispered to Dee, "Hold on."

They went straight up, moving very fast. They went all the way to the sixteenth floor, stopping for a minute to look at the people panic. Some were crying. One guy screamed in our direction, "Get your butt off the top of that thing!" But they really didn't know if someone was on top or not.

Chill unstuck the button and let it drop, then he stopped it real quick. People were pleading, "Please stop." Others were praying not to die. Dee told Chill to stop and let the people off. Chill decided to take them on another ride. It was a fast, scary ride. He went from the first floor to the sixteenth then headed straight back to the first floor.

When they got to the eighth floor, they could see this big, crazy looking thing going the opposite way. Chill told Dee that it was a weight and to never get close to it. It had to have weighed a ton or more. Dee had never seen anything like it, and, when it passed, it took your breath away. They could hear it coming, and when it crossed them on the eighth floor it was like a speeding semi-truck passing you on the highway. It was a little scary but fun. Chill finally stopped on the fourth or fifth floor and opened the door. Everyone ran off. Everyone but the one guy. He was looking hard trying to see if someone was up on top. Dee couldn't hold it any longer, so he burst out laughing at the guy. Chill quickly closed the door as the guy pulled out his gun. This guy was seriously going to shoot up into the dark at them, but the door shut. Chill slapped Dee upside the head and said, "Man, we'd better get off."

Dee learned how to get on top of the elevator without Chill, so he started taking anyone that wanted to go for a ride. Dee took three people on top after getting drunk and smoking weed. More people wanted to go, but when that door opened, and the wind hit them, they got scared and made the right turn.

There was this kid everyone called "Little Man." He could not have been any older than eleven or twelve years old. Dee said, "No, Little Man, get out of here."

As the door was closing, Little Man looked at Dee with his sad, little, cute puppy dog face and said, "Please."

The big door slammed close. Dee stated, "Little Man got more heart than most of these older cats." He opened the door and said, "Come on Little Man." Little Man was all excited and jumped right on. See, when drinking and smoking, most people minds are open to making all kinds of LEFT turns.

Off they went flying from the sixteenth floor to the bottom. With five people on top of the elevator at one time, it was a little crowded. As they were going back up, they could hear the big weight coming closer and closer. When it passed the eighth floor, the big, crazy looking weight came flying by, with a very big breeze. It looked like a monster or something out of a scary movie, especially when you are high. At the seventh floor, Dee looked over at one of his friends, who had his eyes closed and head laid back. He was enjoying the breeze. Riding on top of the elevators made them feel like they were at Disney World or somewhere special. Everyone wanted a way out of the projects, and this was one way of escaping reality.

As they passed the seventh floor, Dee jumped over and pulled Little Man vigorously by his shirt. They froze in shock watching the weight go flying by. They knew that Dee had just saved Little Man's life. At that moment, everyone wanted to take a RIGHT turn. They hollered, "Stop, let me off!" They got off and promised to never go on top again. Little Man gave Dee a hug as the tears ran down his face. One of the other guys who also had tears in his eyes said, "Man, we just saw Little Man's death, all it took was one more second and he was dead. Dee, you saved his life."

Later that summer, Dee had another encounter with Little Man. It was a sunny, 85 degree day, with wind perfect for a softball game. Dee's team had just made the third out and was running up to start their turn at bat. Before the first batter got up to bat, Little Man appeared. It was like he just fell out of the sky. He was drunk, smelling like a straight alcoholic. He had a joint in his mouth, as he stood there with the bat, acting like he was playing. Both teams were telling him to get out the way. Dee went up to Little Man and walked him off the field. Little Man went to sit on the bench but fell and scratched his face up.

Dee said, "Man, you're bleeding. Maybe you should go home and lay down."

Little Man got mad and said, "Screw all of you fake gangbangers." Dee pushed him in the face then pulled him up and pushed him away from them. Little Man staggered away screaming obscenities. "I hate you Dee", he said as he left.

Dee felt sorry for Little Man. He was so young but had no life. This was it, Robert Taylor Homes, the land of no opportunity. Young people couldn't get a job, but they could become a gangbanger, get guns, drugs and or alcohol. They made the best of what they had and lived the best they could in these prison-like walls. Dee felt like Little Man would probably live and die right there in the projects, never to see that there was a life outside of those buildings.

Dee's team had won the game. so they decided to go buy something to drink and some weed. Yes, this was their everyday thing to look forward to - getting high.

As Dee and his friends were hanging out, they heard a woman screaming hysterically. They turned around and saw that it was Little Man's mother. When she saw Dee standing at the end of the building where they hung out, she ran towards him, crying and screaming. They couldn't tell what she was saying, but they knew that she was really mad.

As she ran up to Dee, she swung a baseball bat, hitting Dee in the face. Dee's nose started squirting blood as he pulled his gun out. Everyone knew that you didn't hurt or kill someone's mother. Dee's buddies grabbed him and the gun, as others pushed the mom away. Things seemed to happen so fast, Dee had no idea what was going on. As they pushed her off to her building, Little Man's mom was crying and sobbed, "Dee killed my baby." Looking back at Dee, she screamed, "You murderer!"

Dee looked at his buddies with a lost look on his face. They all looked lost. Moments later the police came, handcuffed Dee and took him to jail. Dee kept asking, "What did I do?" He got no response from the two officers.

Once at the station, they didn't take him to the jail. They took him to a small room, took the cuffs off and told him to take a seat. Dee asked "Shouldn't I have a lawyer here? I'm a minor so where are my parents?"

They said, "Relax Mr. Smart Man. You're not in any trouble. We know that you were not there, but you may have information that we can use. Do you know who had the tool to get on top of the elevators?"

Dee said, "I don't know anything about that."

The officer said, "Are you sure? Did you know your buddy, Little Man is dead?"

Dee was shocked and asked, "What do you mean he is dead? I just saw him."

"Well," the officer explained, "we heard that he was on top of the elevator drunk and high. The weight came down and took Little Man down with it. Yes, Mr. Dee, he's very dead. The coroner is still trying to find all of his body parts. We believe that whoever was up there with him should have stopped the elevator. If they would have he may still be alive. But they got off and left it running, and when it went back down to the first floor, it smashed Little Man to the point where they are finding body parts everywhere."

Dee felt so sorry, knowing that he started this kid riding on top of the elevators and felt like he was responsible for his friend taking that left turn.

Dee never got on top of the elevators again, but it didn't bring Little Man back.

Chapter 4 - **The Fight**

4950 South State Street
Chicago IL.
Enter at your own risk.

"Hey Shorty." I turned around to see one of my partners walking up.

"What's up?" I replied.

"Nothing. Did you know they killed your cousin's friend in that fight you guys had the other night?"

"What... wow," I said. "That kid was just trying to stop them all from jumping my cousin. The kid wasn't a gangbanger, he was a track star who didn't deserve to die in a fight."

I'm mad, sad, and hurt all at once, knowing that it could have been me. For a second I wished it would have been me instead of an innocent kid. See, I was the gangbanger. I ran away from home at a very young age and joined a gang, willingly.

You could say that I was a kid with a serious attitude problem. I was an angry kid who just didn't care about you, your mother, or your kids. It was a sad place to be in life. But at that point in my life, I wanted to kill something or someone.

I was just one of thousands of lost, angry kids. We didn't know much about right turns in life. All we knew were left turns. Everyone was making lefts so why shouldn't we? We were really a bunch of lost kids with nowhere to turn and no one to turn to.

***

I'm Shorty. At times I hated my life and everything about it. I was very angry at having to move to the south side of Chicago and into the projects. As we were moving in, I wanted to take off and just run away. I wanted to cry.

I missed my old neighborhood. I looked up at the sixteen floor red brick building. I saw the gangbangers walking around. I knew some of the guys from past visits. I didn't want to live there, but I had no other choice. At that time, I hated my mother for this.

See, I was a kid when we moved into the Robert Taylor Homes, one of the worst housing projects in Chicago. My grandmother and other family lived there. We always visited them but I never imagined that we would be moving into such a screwed up place. I felt like we were moving into a prison. I had been in these buildings hundreds of time before, but never looked at them the way I was looking today as we were moving into them. They had sixteen floors with ten apartments on each floor. There were red and white buildings going down State Street as far as the eye could see. The smell of urine was so strong you could almost taste it. There were two elevators in each building that almost never worked. People clapped sometimes when they saw that they were working.

Walking up the stairs was the norm. We lived on the fifteenth floor, so that was a lot of stairs. Some nights you would get so far up and start walking into darkness. You could walk up three to four floors in total darkness from people busting out the lights. It was very scary, so you walked up very slowly, hoping not to step into anything.

***

I remember being too young to have a driver's license, but I had a car. It was a big red Ford LTD. One night as I drove up to the building, I saw a big crowd of people. I got all excited, so I quickly parked the car and jumped out to go see what was going on. Before I could get to it, another fight was breaking out.

Fights were the highlights of the projects. There was a least one fight a day, and on hot summer days there could be two or three fights going on all at once. It was like you didn't know which one to run to. You really wanted to see them all, not missing anything. There was something about fights that really excited people. As I pushed and pulled my way to the front, I saw that it was some punks, from the white buildings, down here starting fights. I didn't know these guys, but I knew that they were gang members.

Two guys were locked up with each other, like two pit bulls. They were holding each other very tightly, sweating, and breathing very hard. I thought they must have been fighting for some time, because it looked like they were both tired and were trying to get a quick rest before fighting more. Once they broke loose, I saw that it was my cousin, Tee. Tee was one of my favorite cousins. He was a very light skinned, pretty boy, who refused to join a gang. The girls loved him, but a lot of the girls were the girlfriends of gangbangers. Right away, I thought that this fight had to be over a girl because Tee didn't mess with no one. He was this happy go lucky kid that had no problems with people. I also knew, from growing up as cousins, he could fight, and he wasn't a punk. I saw him before he saw me. I could see in his eyes that he was a little scared, because these guys weren't from our building, and they were gangbangers. They were from the white buildings, which was about two blocks away.

There had to be at least fifty of them all around this fight. Tee knew that if you're not a gangbanger, which he wasn't, but fighting a gangbanger, which he was, then you'd better not win that fight. He also knew that you probably didn't want to win that fight, because, if you were lucky, they wouldn't just all start beating the mess out of you, just for fun. If you're not a banger, you have no backup. Most people won't get involved with a neutron, which was what we called a person that wasn't a banger. My cousin Tee was a neutron, and he knew he was in trouble.

Once Tee saw me, he instantly got confidence. I watched him change and was ready to kick this dude's butt. He went from fear of being jumped, to hearing me holler, "Get him Cuzzo." Cuzzo was something we started calling each other, because we had a lot of cousins. So the boys started calling each other Cuzzo.

I'm not sure of the year, but it was the time when LL Cool J wore the big chain around his neck. Everyone had big silver chains, some had gold and thought they were all that. Maybe they were all that, or maybe I was jealous, because I had a big chain too. See, I had a real big chain. Like something you would lock your bike up with. Yes, I wore my chain around my neck with a big lock on the end locking it together. I thought I was cool.

Cuzzo was beating this tough guy so bad that the tough guy grabbed him. By now they were both tired and holding each other in a bear hug. They were really trying to catch their breath. Out of nowhere, some dude from the crowd swings really hard like he was trying to break something. He hit my Cuzzo in his ribs. Instantly, without thinking, I took that chain and lock from around my neck and busted the dude upside his head. He looked me dead in my eyes as he fell back. I thought I had just killed another kid. It all happened so fast. I looked up at one of my fellow gangbangers as he shook his head, saying, "You shouldn't done that man." I knew that I had just made one of the biggest mistakes ever. Even though I didn't know the guys, they were members of the same gang. I should not have done that.

First thing hit my mind was running, so I did. That was the next worst thing I did that night. I ran through one building trying to make it to my uncle's building, which was the next building over. I was always dressed up, so it wasn't any surprise when I looked down at my shoes. I was running for my life in Stacy Adams shoes. I knew that if anyone was chasing me, they would have on gym shoes. As I was approaching my uncle's building, I took a look back, still running, I didn't see but two or three people chasing me. I felt better now as I was fast and had enough of a lead on them that once I hit that hallway it was over, I'm gone. My uncle lived on the fourteenth floor, and I would have to run up most, if not all fourteen floors, before they stopped chasing me.

My heart was pumping fast. The only thing left was to make it over this four foot wall and into the hallway, and I'm free. As I approached the wall, I looked and saw so many people running around the side of the building trying to cut me off. I knew it was a dangerous choice but I didn't have many. So I ran faster and harder. I felt like I was floating on air. I had to run right pass all these guys to get to the hallway. I was really scared now because we were all running in the same direction where we would have to cross each other like an X. If I make it first, I win. But if I don't, I lose. So I ran with everything I had. Everything was moving fast, but I had only two things on my mind. One, what would happen if they caught me, and two, if I made it to the hall would they continue to chase me? I knew if I did make it to the hallway, I wouldn't have the energy to go up the stairs. My mind was going crazy. I was scared because these guys didn't know me. I later found out that the guy I knocked out with my lock and chain was their leader.

I had never felt this way before. I was truly running for my life. I'd been in this situation before, but never the victim. I used to run track, so I saw the wall closing in on me. Jumping it would be like being on the track field. It's just that I never ran track in a pair of Stacy Adams. As I took the leap into the air, I could tell that I would beat them to the hallway. I felt like I got a second wind or drank a super speed juice or something. I started feeling less worried as I cleared that wall.

"Oh no," I thought." Please, God, no, as the tip of my pointy toe shoe hit the wall. I was running so fast that I flipped before I hit the ground hard. Before I even stopped rolling, I started feeling what I was running so hard to get away from. I will never forget that first kick to my face, another in my ribs, and before I knew it, I was starting to feel pain all over my body. All I could do was lay there and cover my face. I tried to get up, but every time I moved I got it from somewhere else. I started blacking out thinking, "I can't die like this." I prayed, "God, if you're real, please, please show me now." But nothing happened.

I started trying harder to get up, but every time I moved I continued to get knocked back down. All of a sudden, I felt this sharp pain in my head. I knew that I was about to die, right here, right now. It was hard to believe that I was being beaten to death by a gang that I had given my life to. I thought about the time when my family said that I wouldn't live to see eighteen if I didn't start living right. This was the reason my mom wanted me out the projects, but I never saw this coming.

I felt something warm and thick running down my face; my body was starting to break down. I started feeling paralyzed and then I realized that it was blood, my blood, running down my face. They had stabbed me not once but three times in my head with pocket knives. All I could do was pray to God, knowing that I was about to die. I could feel bats and golf clubs hitting me all over my body. I got as comfortable as I could get in this situation, waiting for that last blow, the one that would take my life.

Just when I had given up and accepted the fact that I was about to die, I heard a very loud, strong voice screaming, "Get up, man, get up." I realized that the hitting became less and less, until there was no one hitting me anymore. I got one eye clear enough from the blood to see that it was a family friend with a steel milk crate. He was swinging it like he would kill anyone that came near.

"Come on, Shorty, get up," he screamed.

I tried but couldn't. He hollered, "Get up now!" He tried pulling my arm as I gave it my all. I could tell that any minute these guys would start beating both of us up. We managed to get me up, and we started running slowly towards my uncle's building. He kept saying, "Come on." As bad as I wanted to stop, he would not let me. The pain was running all over my body as we ran up the stairs.

We ran all the way to the ninth floor, where my aunt lived. My heart was pumping really hard, my head was spinning, and I needed water badly. Once we hit the ninth floor, I took a deep breath and collapsed face first onto the concrete floor. I had no control, as my body went down in slow motion. The last thing I felt was my face hitting that ice cold floor. I was out.

The next time I opened my eyes, I knew I had died and gone to heaven. I tried looking harder, as it seemed like it was just bright light all over. It was white walls and beautiful nurses in white uniforms. I would have smiled if I could have.

Suddenly, sadness came on me as I thought, "Wow, I didn't want to die at such a young age." Then I turned and saw my black uncle standing there. I wasn't sure if I was happy or sad, knowing that I wasn't dead. Even though I didn't want to die, I liked the idea of being in heaven with those beautiful nurses.

Whatever they gave me at that hospital worked, because even though my arm was in a sling, I had fractured ribs, and stitches in my head, I felt no pain. I was angry, hurt that my own gang did this to me. I was also worried about my cousin, hoping that he was all right. When I got back to the projects, people told me how the gang had beaten my cousin badly and beat his friend to death. I thought that could have been me. I was angry.

Shortly after I got out of the hospital, I went to see the family of the kid that got killed. His brother and a couple more guys were in the back room getting ready to go shoot whoever they thought killed his little brother. I told him to give me a gun. We went back to the building where this all had happened, but none of the guys were around. We started shooting like crazy, everyone started running for cover. I hollered, "Where you all at now?" It was four of us out there shooting. It was like a war going on without the enemy being there.

I realized how stupid we looked. At that moment, something hit me. I looked at the guys I was shooting with, and said, "Man, I can't live like this anymore. I'm tired of watching kids die over nothing. These projects are full of left turns, everyone's taking them. I'm done. Your little brother was murdered, my cousin and I were almost murdered, and I hate this life. My brother has been trying to get me to come to Minneapolis for months. I got to get out of here; I can't live this life anymore. I'm going to Minnesota and try to live a better life."

Chapter 5 - **LOVE AND HATE**

Dan and Ronda were the kind of couple that made you feel good just being around them. From the outside, they looked like the perfect couple, and they knew it.

It all started one day when Dan and his brother, Ty, were working on Dan's car. This tall, beautiful, slim woman came walking down the alley with her dog. Dan stated to his brother, "Look at that sexy woman coming down the alley." You could tell she had just gotten off work; she had on this beautiful red, blue, and green flowered summer dress that blew perfectly with the nice breeze. Her face had been made up so that she was glowing in the sun. As she came down the alley, looking like a scene from "America's Next Top Model," Dan started singing a song, "There goes my baby." As she was about to walk by, Dan stopped her and started talking to her, not really knowing what to say to such a beautiful woman. As he continued opening his mouth, it seemed like the words were coming from somewhere else, and they were coming out very smoothly. Ronda took a liking to Dan as she took his number and continued walking her dog. Dan was smiling from ear to ear, telling his brother, "Man, I'm in love."

Ronda called Dan the next evening and offered him a drink. Dan didn't know that Ronda lived in the house right next door. They started seeing each other daily, going out dancing, movies, dinners and nights on the lake. They were really falling for one another. One night they decided to go dancing. The music was great, and they danced all night long.

Dan was a stepper from Chicago. When he stepped it was like he was in another world. Ronda was from Minneapolis and loved to dance. Dan taught her how to step, and she followed like water flowing down the river. When they danced you would feel the happiness they felt as they glided around the dance floor together.

What Dan didn't know was that Ronda was a big flirt. Ronda didn't know that Dan had abandonment issues and was a very jealous man. Ronda smiled and said goodbye to a guy she knew as they were leaving the club. Dan didn't like it and asked "What was that all about?" She smiled at him and before she could stop smiling Dan slapped her in her face. Ronda was not a punk, she slapped him back. As much as they loved each other, when alcohol came into the picture their love could quickly turn into hate. They truly loved each other and tried everything to fix the one major broken part of their relationship, alcohol. They tried to stop drinking but soon were back on the bottle. Dan even got them into couple's therapy and for some time it seemed to have been working for them. They had been together for about three years. The more they would drink, the worse their fights became.

Dan knew that because of his drinking and jealousy, he was starting to lose the love of his life. Dan had lived most of his life making left turns and was trying to start living right. He felt like his life was almost perfect except that he was a jealous alcoholic.

Ronda had a birthday coming up, and Dan wanted to do something special for her but didn't know what. Ronda and Dan were running late for dinner with Ronda's Aunt Cathy, who was looked to as the matriarch of the family. Other family members included Ronda's sister Lisa, who seemed to be very nice but didn't say much, Ronda's son Tim, who is a tall, slim, pretty boy, and Ronda's two beautiful nieces. They all met at this really nice, expensive restaurant. Before they knew it, everyone was laughing, talking about everything from the weather to the nieces' new boyfriends. They made jokes and talked about each other.

This place had a very big fireplace and soft mellow smooth jazz playing in the background. There was bright red carpet all over the floor, making the place a little exciting. Ronda got up from the table, which was made of fine oak wood. One could tell that whoever owned this place spent plenty of money getting it to look the way it did. While Ronda excused herself from the table, her sister and aunt asked Dan, "So, what are you going to do for Ronda's birthday?" Dan didn't know. He hadn't made any plans but felt like he better say something. Dan was feeling like he had been put on the spot, like a kid in a candy store getting caught stealing candy. Or more like a deer caught at night by a car's headlights. His mind was going crazy trying to figure out what to say, and then it hit him, like a flash of lights. He opened his mouth but felt like nothing was coming out. He felt paralyzed as he saw Ronda returning from the restroom. Dan still didn't know what to say or do. Knowing he had to say something, all of a sudden it came out like a long slow motion picture. His words were slurring or something and coming out very slowly as he said, "I'm giving her a surprise party." Right away he felt like slapping himself upside the head for saying that. What was he thinking? He knew he had never given anyone a surprise party. After seeing the excitement on everyone's face around the table about the surprise party, he knew he had to go through with it. Everyone was excited and extra happy about this party. Everyone but Dan, he wasn't excited at all. He just faked it. He felt pretty bad but continued with his fake smile.

After dinner everyone went their separate ways. As Ronda and Dan drove home, she asked Dan why everyone was acting so secretive. Dan saw his way out of this party but didn't take it. He wanted to tell her what happened and wanted her to help him fix it. Instead he acted like he didn't know what she was talking about, not wanting to let everyone down. After seeing everyone glow with excitement, he had to have this party. Ronda started making Dan mad on their ride home, talking about how she didn't like him having secrets with her family. She wanted to know what was going on. By the time they got home, Dan was ready to say forget it and tell her everything. He knew then he would not have to give her a party and would save a lot of money.

The next day Dan decided to go through with the party, so he got started. First, he took one of Ronda's old pictures; it was a picture with her smiling so bright. He took the picture to a photo shop and had them blow it up to the size of a poster. He liked it so much that he made ten copies. Next, he went and got all kinds of decorations: streamers, balloons, strings and all. He found a place in the basement to hide everything. A place where he knew she would never go, it was spooky and dark. It had spider webs and dust all over. He cleaned a spot and started hiding things there for days until the day of her birthday.

Dan used to buy, fix, and resale cars. Over the next couple weeks he sold maybe ten cars, that gave him plenty money to pull this off. Dan had Tim and Dan's daughter Cindy, a beautiful, respectable young lady, help keep things in order. Dan's plan was to have this party in their backyard, but he wasn't sure if the weather would be nice. Hey, it's Minnesota so it could be cold, hot, rainy, or snowy. As the days got closer to Ronda's birthday, Dan found himself running around like a chicken with its head cut off. He wasn't getting much sleep, up early mornings gladly driving Ronda to work so that he could get back to the plan. He seemed so calm and relaxed until she got out the car and went into her job. As soon as she got out the car, Dan was off to the races running in over drive trying to get things done. Dan was very nervous and worried, hoping everything turned out right. He decided that if he was going to give her a surprise party, it would be the best she ever had.

It was finally the day of her birthday. Dan woke her up making sure she went to work. That was hard because Ronda kept saying, "It's my birthday. So maybe I will just call in and take the day off."

Dan was sweating bullets, he told her that he had plans for her birthday, and the place they were going was by her job. He asked her to go to work dressed up nice so that they could go right after she got off. He asked her to please go to work, and said he would even drive her and pick her up. She loved it when he took her to work, so she went. Dan thought, "Wow, that was a close call."

After dropping her off, he was again off to the races. He purchased a keg of beer and all kinds of the biggest bottles of drinks he could find. He spent hundreds of dollars at the liquor store. He went and purchased meat by the cases. He was running in and out of the house telling Tim and Cindy what he wanted them to start doing. It was crunch time, last minute prep. Dan had Tim, Cindy, and all their friends take everything out of the hiding place and start decorating the house, the yard, and the garage. They asked him how he was going to get Ronda home without her seeing all the people, cars, and decorations. Dan smiled and stated, "Let me worry about that part. When I call you guys around 5:15, have everyone in the back yard and in the garage."

The weather turned out wonderful. It was a bright day with blue skies, sunny, with no clouds. It was a perfect summer day. You could even smell the mums blooming in the yard. It was time to go pick up Ronda from work. Everything was going great. Dan had sent e-mails, invitations in the mail, and made phone calls to all her friends, her family, and his family. Dan started the grill and let Tim take charge of the meat. They set up drinks in the house, yard, and in the garage where he had tables and chairs set up for people who might want to play cards and or smoke. Dan had music playing and put speakers outside, in the house and in the garage. He felt ready, still nervous, but ready. Dan was very nervous as he picked Ronda up from work. He gave her a big kiss and said, "Happy birthday, baby. Are you ready for a great day?" Dan stopped the car, as he fearfully patted his pockets, he stated, "Sorry baby, we have to stop at home. I forgot my wallet." He promised it would only take a minute.

As they got closer to the house Dan could feel his heart beating so loud, he was afraid Ronda might hear it. He was a mess on the inside but stayed cool and calm, not wanting her to get any idea. Dan stopped at the corner store one block from home and secretly called Tim and Cindy telling them to get everyone into the garage and back yard. Dan drove the opposite way down the alley so that Ronda wouldn't see all the cars or people before the surprise.

As they pulled closer to the garage, Dan pushed the garage door opener as if he was going to drive into the garage. As the door slowly opened they saw feet and legs, then many more feet and legs, tables, chairs, decorations and then faces. It was packed with people everywhere. Dan cut the car off and looked over at Ronda. He could see the tears of happiness and how shocked she was. Dan was shocked also because he had just left the house, and no one was there. Then he remembered that on the invitations it stated the time to be there for the surprise, and they were all there. As they got out of the car and started making their way through the garage and into the yard, it was more of a surprise to see so many smiling faces. Everyone seemed happy.

After looking over at Ronda and seeing her happier than he had ever seen her, Dan took a deep breath, and for once in the last few weeks, he could finally relax. He grabbed a very large glass, some ice, and a bottle of Hennessey and sat back. Dan was feeling like it was his birthday or something. He watched as people danced, clapped, and sang to the music. Dan hollered out, "I did it," as he danced his way to the house.

The great smell of ribs, onions, and corn on the cob filled the air. There were smiling faces everywhere you looked. Ronda had friends there that she hadn't seen in years. Ronda's uncle was there. He never went to birthday parties. He was from northern Minnesota. He had the long, gray beard, blue overalls, and long hair in a ponytail.

Dan was feeling good about pulling this party off. It really touched him when he looked up and saw the uncle grooving, patting his feet and shaking his head, trying to keep up with the music. Uncle was having a great time and looking good doing it. Dan grabbed Ronda's hand and started dancing with her in the backyard. Everyone was watching as they put their moves on. Her friends were surprised to see her dancing so freely. They started saying, "Will the real Ronda please stand up?"

Dan started to drink a little more than usual. He was standing there thinking, "It gets no better than this." Then it hit him. Dan grabbed his buddy, who lived three houses down the alley. He was hiding Ronda's present in his friend's garage. Dan put the present in his own garage then went to find Tim. Dan had Tim keep his mom's attention while he got her present into the backyard. When people saw the gift, their mouths dropped. Once Dan got it set where he wanted it, he told people to go tell Tim to bring his mom out back. When she turned to come out the back door, there Dan was, sitting on her brand new red and orange scooter. Dan had wrapped a big, pink bow around it. Ronda had always wanted a scooter. Everyone was surprised including Ronda. Dan hollered, "Come on, baby, check it out." She was smiling from ear to ear with tears of happiness in her eyes.

Ronda got onto the back, and they rode in circles around the yard. Everyone was taking pictures like Dan and Ronda were super stars or something. As they rode around the yard Ronda whispered in his ear, "This is the best birthday ever. I love you." Dan felt like he was going to melt like butter. Everyone saw how happy they were together on her special day. Dan looked around and felt so proud for making this day so wonderful.

As the evening grew late, Dan continued to drink. He drank so much that he actually passed out for a while.

"Wake up, man, wake up," one of the guests said as he woke Dan up. Dan opened his eyes slowly, as he was still feeling the effects of the alcohol. Dan recognized the guy as someone he knew that was jealous of him. He always suspected that this guy had a thing for Ronda. He didn't remember inviting him to the party but, as neighborhood parties go, when free food and booze are involved no telling who will show up at your house, invited or not.

"Man," Dan said as he tried to sit up. "Why are you here? You had better not be trying to get up on my woman."

"Don't worry about me. You'd better be worried about the guy your woman is riding around on her new scooter," the guy said as he laughed and walked away.

Dan couldn't believe it. He jumped up and grabbed his liquor. He took a swallow and started walking through the house hoping to see Ronda before he got outside. But he didn't, and when he saw that her scooter was gone, he got really mad. He tried to play it off, but when you're drunk, you're drunk. Dan jumped into his truck, with the bottle in his hand, and started driving fast down the alley. When he got to the corner he saw a light coming towards him from a distance. Dan thought, "That's her and she better not have nobody on that scooter." As he got closer he could see that she had someone riding with her. How dare her to embarrass him like this. Dan was angry, but he was really feeling hurt, jealous, and drunk. As he drove towards Ronda coming at him on her scooter, he decided that he was going to teach her, and whoever this guy was, a lesson.

As they came within half a block, Dan decided that he was going to scare them. He drove into their lane then came back over. He hit the gas hard and turned back at her. This time, when he turned at her, his alcohol flipped over and started pouring out. Dan reached fast to grab his bottle. As he reached for that bottle, he heard a crunch sound and he thought that it didn't sound good. It was like hitting a bump in the road. He prayed to God that what he just heard was not what his mind was thinking.

Dan had just run over the love of his life, her cousin, and the new scooter. Ronda and her cousin were killed instantly. Dan got life in prison. He ended up losing his mind after a year and hung himself.

The kids, family, and friends all lost three great people on that special day. All because Dan was addicted to a life of left turns and couldn't get it right.

Chapter 6 – **Eddie: Kid with a Gun**

Eddie was the kid that always had a gun on him and wasn't afraid to use it. He was still in elementary school when he decided that he was not going to stay in school. Eddie dropped out and started gangbanging and selling drugs. He had everyone afraid of him. Eddie and his dad got into an argument when his dad said something that hurt Eddie's feelings. Eddie pulled out a gun in front of everyone and shot his dad. After that everyone, including adults, was afraid of him.

Eddie heard about a guy trying to help kids stop taking left turns in life and start taking rights. Eddie thought this was a joke, living in the projects, taking rights when all his life it was all about lefts. Eddie had a chance to talk with the guy doing all this talk about rights. He got into an argument with him and pulled his gun on the guy. Everyone started running and hiding, but the guy started saying things like, "Lord, please help Eddie. He's hurting right now and has plenty reasons to be angry." He continued saying, "Please allow Eddie to see life in a different way, and please show him that he can put guns down and live a happy life. In Jesus' name."

To everyone's surprise Eddie said, "Amen" and handed over his gun, as the tears ran down his face.

The next week Eddie was back in school, passing every test he took. He cut his hair and started dressing nice. Eddie even backed away from his gang. Eddie couldn't believe how smart he was. He started going to church, stopped doing drugs, and never picked up a gun again. Eddie made it. He started loving life on the right side of the tracks.

Chapter 7 — **Terry: The Wanna-be Gangbanger**

Terry was one of those kids that just wanted to fit in somewhere. He wasn't getting the love he wanted from home, so he decided to join a gang. There, he felt the love he always wanted, so he thought. Terry knew in his heart that he wasn't a tough guy but never wanted anyone to know. Most of the older guys saw right through him and made him feel like he was a part of things but used him to do things they didn't want to do. We used to call that kind of guy a "sendoff," because they used to send him off to snatch women's purses, rob a store, or go get their weed. But you couldn't tell him that he was being used.

Terry was told to go rob a store. When he got to the store, he wanted to change his mind, but thought that if he didn't do it he may be kicked out the gang or even beat up. They sent another guy with him. As soon as Terry pulled his guns out, people came out of the back and side doors of the store with very big guns.

As they were on their way to jail, Terry started looking like he wanted to cry. His friend told him to stop. He said, "Man, look, you are a juvenile, and they are not going to do nothing to you. You may get out today, but because it's Friday, you may not get out until Monday." He also said that he was on probation, so Terry should say that his buddy didn't know anything about this robbery. He went on the say, "Terry, man, you know that if anything did go wrong, we all would be there for you. You know we will keep money on your books and visit all the time. But you'll be all right. You don't have a criminal record. So what can they do to you?"

Once they arrived at the police station, Terry and his buddy were taken into separate rooms for questioning. Terry told the officers that it was all his idea and that his buddy knew nothing about him robbing the store. After about an hour, Terry saw his buddy getting released. His buddy was smiling, giving Terry the thumbs up as he walked past the glass window. His buddy said something, but Terry couldn't hear him through the thick glass. He knew whatever it was, it was positive, and that he would be getting released and back on the streets with his real family, back playing his role as a tough guy. Terry sat back in his chair, waiting for the officers to come release him.

The two officers returned to the room and told Terry to stand up and put his hands behind his back. Terry couldn't believe it. He was really going to jail. He called a couple of his gang family and was told to just hang in there. They told him that he would be out Monday.

The judge decided that he was going to make an example of Terry and gave him six months in jail. Terry hurried back to call his buddies, but most of them had changed their numbers. He did get in touch with one of the guys and was happy to hear that they were going to send him money. A couple weeks later, he tried calling to see if anyone of them would visit, but to his surprise, everyone had changed their numbers. He was sad. He checked his mail every day, and he never received anything from any of them. His cellmate called him stupid and stated, "Boy, when you go to jail, you're on your own, the gang don't care about you. Look at all you did for them. They haven't visited, they haven't sent you any money, and they won't even write you a letter. Terry, you better start trying to live your life right and stop taking left turns in life. Man, call your real family. You only get one mom and dad. Learn to love them for who they are." Terry called his family.

The next day, Terry's mom, dad, sister, and brother were there to visit him. Terry continued getting visits from his family. He received a letter from them with a hundred dollars for him to buy things. He never heard from his gang. Terry went to school while in jail, he got released and continued school. He graduated and went off to college. He ended up with a job and never looked back.

Terry went back to visit the old neighborhood and was surprised to see that most of his old gang friends were still there: drinking, smoking, and gangbanging. He was told that the guy he went to jail for had been killed trying to rob someone. Terry realized that because he stopped smoking weed, drinking, doing crimes, and gangbanging, his life changed. Terry, for the first time in his life, was making right turns and loving it.

Chapter 8 - **Big Will: The Bully**

Big Will was a cool little, guy until he turned fourteen. It seemed like overnight his life changed. He stood 5' 11" and weighed 250 pounds. One day Big Will was at school and realized that he didn't have money for lunch. He jokingly went into his friend's pocket and took his money. His friend had $24. Big Will realized that his friend didn't even try to put up a fight for his money, so Will gave his friend $10 and took the rest. He told his friend that he would give it back, but they both knew that he wouldn't.

Big Will started smoking weed, and when he didn't have it, he would get depressed and would stay in his room. He came out when he was hungry or when he had the munchies. One day he saw a pizza in the fridge and decided to eat the whole pizza. When his mom came home, she complained and told him that it was his brother's pizza and asked him why he had to eat all of it. He snapped on his mom for the first time. She was shocked and didn't know what to do.

A few minutes later, his brother came home and was screaming about people eating all his food. Big Will came out of his room and hit his brother in the mouth. Blood started shooting all over their kitchen. Their mother came out and told Will to get out of her house. She took his brother to the hospital where he received ten stitches in his lip. On their way home, he asked his mom, "What's wrong with Will? He used to be so nice to people. Kids at school are afraid of him, and I'm starting to hate him."

Big Will started smoking weed daily and started taking kid's money right out of their hands and would dare them to say something. Most people walked away, some cried, and when people did say something, he would try knocking them out with one punch. He quickly had most people afraid of him, no one liked him anymore and they would do whatever they could to avoid him.

One day there was a knock at the door. When Will's mom opened the door, she was pushed aside by some guys she had never seen before. As they came into her house, they started looking in all the rooms as if they were looking for someone.

Will's mom and brother were very afraid, as they held each other, wondering what they were looking for. The guys all came together and pushed the mom and son down on the couch. One of the guys took out his gun and sat it on the table right in front of them. He said "You tell that big, dumb kid of yours that if he ever takes another penny from my kid or any other kid in our neighborhood, we will be back. We will take him away, and you will never see him again."

Will's mom called everyone and went everywhere she thought he may have gone, hoping to find her son before they did. It was late now, and his mom couldn't sleep. She prayed that nothing had happened to her son.

Big Will finally came home around 1 am. When his mom heard the door close she thanked Jesus. When she came out the room, she was crying and went to hug Will, but he was high and drunk. He pushed her off of him. She told him what had happened and that he was not only putting his life in danger but his family's life was in danger also.

Will acted like he wasn't afraid of anything or anyone. He asked who they were, and he got scared when she couldn't tell him who they were. She did say that they were not kids, and they were not playing. "These people will kill you, baby, she said." I already called your grandma, and we decided to have you go stay with her for the summer. School will be out in a week. You should start packing, because I'm getting your ticket tomorrow and you're leaving as soon as school is over."

Big Will was on the Greyhound, on his way to the country. Will knew that his granddad didn't play his games and would have him working on his farm. Once there, his granddad told him the rules and stated that he better not bring that city stuff to his little country town. He told Will that he was going to teach him how to drive a tractor and have him plow the fields. He said that he would pay him as much as he paid his other guys. Big Will liked the idea of being in the country, away from the city, and having his first job. He also felt that his getting away may have saved his life.

Big Will met a guy named Charles, who also drove a tractor for his granddad. Charles was a smaller guy. He was a couple of years older than Will, but they got along great. One evening after work, Charles took Will to the local hangout. This was a place, by the lake, where everyone came to relax, swim, have fun, drink, or whatever. Will was looking at a girl standing in the water, she was looking back at him too. Will was thinking, "Wow she's beautiful." He said, "Charles, look at that girl in the water. She keeps looking back at me."

Charles stated, "She may like you, go say hello."

Big Will didn't want to tell Charles that he had never had a girlfriend, and that he didn't even know how to talk to a girl.

Charles said, "You want to meet her?"

"Man, I wouldn't know what to say to such a woman," Big Will said as he looked away, almost embarrassed.

"Man, it's nothing. I will help you," Charles said in an encouraging way.

As bad as Will wanted to take him up on that, he didn't want to embarrass himself. However, it looked as if he would not have a choice. The young lady started walking towards them. The closer she got to them, the more nervous Big Will got. By the time she reached them, he was sweating all over.

"Hello, I'm Sherry," she said as she held out her hand to shake Will's.

He slowly looked up at her beautiful dark-skinned face. She had on a bikini that showed her long, silky legs. She had long, straight black hair that blew perfectly with the soft wind. Big Will was in a daze. He had never in his life been this close to such a lady.

She looked at Charles with this crazy look. Charles grabbed Will's hand and gently pulled it away from Sherry's. This snapped Big Will back into reality. He smiled at her and apologized for holding her hand so long.

Charles said, "Sherry, this is my friend Will, and Will this is my sister, Sherry."

Sherry could tell that Will liked her, because he got this big, silly smile on his face, his mouth was wide open. He was stuck with nothing to say. Finally he reintroduced himself and said, "I'm in love."

Right away he said, "Oops, I'm sorry." They all started laughing. Sherry sat down next to Will, and they started talking. They cut Charles right out of the conversation. He decided to leave the beach, but Will and Sherry stayed and talked for hours. You could tell that she liked him too.

They had fallen in love over the summer and were inseparable. Big Will taught her how to drive a tractor, and Sherry taught him how to skate. They would double date with Charles and his girlfriend. One night they all went dancing, and to Will's surprise, he was the best dancer out of all of them. He didn't know he could dance. Now he was trying to teach Sherry a couple moves.

Big Will saw how great Charles and his sister got along and wished that he could have that kind of relationship with his family. All three of them started getting sad, because they knew that summer was about to be over, and Big Will would be leaving in about a week. The night before he was to go back home, they talked about all the fun times they had. Will told them that this was the best summer of his life. He asked them to come visit him next year during their spring break. They were both happy to know that they would go to the big city in the spring.

Sherry told him that she wished he didn't have to leave; Will said the same as they hugged. Sherry started to cry. Will asked her to please not cry, as he held back his own tears.

Charles jumped in and said, "Man, I wish you could stay here and go to school with me. I had the best summer ever and wish it didn't have to end." Charles started crying and added, "I can't wait to do it all over again next summer. I love you man." This made Big Will drop a tear or two as they said their final goodbyes.

Big Will was back in the hood. He put back on his bully face and started right back where he had left off, like he didn't care about the guys that said they would kill him.

Big Will and Sherry talked almost daily. She told him how boring it had been since he left. She also told him that her brother really missed him and always talked about how different it would be if he had stayed.

"I don't know what's been wrong with him, he seems a little down and depressed," Sherry confided in him one night on the phone." He doesn't go anywhere or do anything anymore. He just goes to school and then home. That's on the days when he feels like going to school."

Big Will sat there listening, wishing he knew what was wrong with his friend, Charles, wishing there was something he could do to help. He told Sherry that Charles seemed so happy when he was there. Sherry said that it could be because he left. Big Will told her that he would call Charles and see what was going on with him.

"Hello," Charles said as he answered the phone.

"Hey, what's up bro?" Bill Will said, trying to see what he could pick up from Charles' voice.

"Not much," Charles replied, not being his usual talkative self.

"How you been man? I haven't heard from you?" Big Will said as he definitely detected something strange in Charles' voice.

"I'm ok," Charles said as if he was distracted.

"You seem a little down man, are you sure you're ok?" Will replied.

"I'm good. Sometimes I just hate this country town and some of the people here," Charles said as he became a little more engaged in the conversation.

"I know what you mean. Sometimes I hate being in this big city. You know I'm here for you if you ever want to vent, or just talk, all right?"

"Yah, Big Will. Wish you were here. Love you, man," Charles said.

"Love you too, bro. Man, keep your head up, all right?" Will said.

"Ok Will, thanks. Talk to you later, man. Goodbye," Charles said, almost sounding like his old self.

After he hung up the phone, it was business as usual for Big Will. He hit the streets to collect his money. He saw someone who owed him, and he walked up behind him and grabbed him by the throat.

"Let him go, Big Will. Man, he can't breathe," one of the guys said.

Big Will said, "Look sucker, you better have my money tomorrow."

"Okay man I will try," the other stuttered as he rubbed his neck.

A few minutes later Big Will saw someone else. "Hey you, come here. Where is my money?" The guy Big Will was talking to knew not to run. If you made Big Will have to run after you, you were in big trouble. It was always better to just face the music.

"Big Will, I couldn't get it all. I only have $50," the guy mumbled, hoping that this would keep Big Will from slamming him on the ground.

"Give it here," Big Will demanded, as he grabbed the money out of the man's shaking hand. "I want the rest tomorrow, punk."

As Big Will was continuing to walk down the street, he could hear someone call his name. He turned around and saw his little brother running towards him. He could tell that something was wrong.

"Hey Will," his brother hollered as he slowed down, visibly out of breath." Something's wrong with mom. She got off the phone looking like she was ready to cry. She told me to please come find you."

"Tell her I will be there later. I got to get my money from these little punks," Big Will said as he turned around.

"Are you serious?" his brother yelled at him. "Mom is hurting. Anything could be wrong, and all you can think about is bullying people, taking their money. Man, please come home with me. Don't send me back alone and hurt her more. Will, man, we only got one mom, and when she's gone you will hurt for things like this."

"All right little bro, let's go home. I will catch these fools tomorrow."

When they returned to the house, Will asked, "Hey Mom, what's wrong?"

"William, please call your girlfriend."

"Mom, what's going on?"

"I don't know. She just said that she needs you right now. She did say that if you can't get in touch with her, she will call you tonight at 8 pm."

Big Will tried to call her phone. "She's not answering. I can call her brother," he said.

Charles phone rang a few times before his voice mail started. "Hello, hey, I got you. Sorry, this is Charles voice mail, please leave a message."

"What's up baby boy? It's Big Will, give me a call. I'm trying to get in touch with your sister. Miss you man, hope everything's all right in the country world. Talk later."

An hour passed, and Will was still not able to get in touch with anyone. Will was pacing back and forth, calling Sherry's phone then Charles' back to back. He was really worried, because Sherry always answered her phone.

Big Will, his mother, and brother were all sitting there when the phone rang. Big Will answered before the first ring completed." Hello," he said all worried.

"Hi...," Sherry couldn't say anything else before she broke down in tears.

"Hey, hey, what's wrong baby? Why didn't you answer your phone?" Will said, extremely worried at this point.

"I couldn't answer it here in the hospital," she said.

"What hospital? Are you alright? What happened?" Will screamed.

"It's Charles... he's dead," Sherry said as she began to cry again.

"Noooooooooooo!" Will screamed. "Who did this? I swear when I find them..."

"He did it!" Sherry screamed." Charles killed himself. He committed suicide."

Big Will held the phone, dazed. His mother gently guided him to the chair. Will felt like he was in the twilight zone. His attention finally came back to his conversation on the phone.

"...been asking me for money lately. I stopped giving it to him, thinking he was on drugs," Sherry was saying. "He killed himself because a bully at school was threatening to humiliate him in front of his girlfriend if he didn't have his money tomorrow."

"Oh my God, I'm so sorry. I'm so very sorry. Please God forgive me," Big Will said as he fell from the chair to his knees. His mom picked up the phone and told Sherry that Will would have to call her back later. His mom did not hear all of the conversation, but she could hear Shelly when she screamed Charles was dead.

Big Will was feeling like he was that same bully that just killed his girlfriend's brother. Will broke down when it hit him that his best friend was dead, and that his girlfriend was suffering from such a great loss. He never had a clue of how his bullying was hurting everyone.

The next few weeks were very hard for Big Will, Sherry and her family. However, through all of the pain that Big Will felt, he was able to come to a life changing decision. He remembered the pastor at Charles' funeral say that the blame for this does not just rest with the ones that bullied Charles. He said that every person that bullies someone else is to blame. He even went as far as to randomly point people out in the congregation. The pastor pointed at a middle aged lady and said, "Have you been a bully? If so, you help put Charles here." He then pointed at a some girls that were sitting in the back. "Have you ladies bullied anyone before? Talking about their weight or how their hair looked. If so, you help put Charles here." Then the pastor pointed at Big Will." Have you every bullied someone before? Took their lunch money or picked on someone for being smaller than you? If so, you help put Charles here. "

The words stabbed Big Will in his heart like a knife. Luckily the pastor asked everyone to bow their heads in prayer at that moment. That gave Big Will a moment to breath. He thought about all the families he had affected with his bullying. He asked God to heal this family and all the other families affected by bullies like himself. Will then asked God to change his life. Big Will decided at that moment that he would never ever bully another kid again.

Big Will started volunteering at a kids' club helping kids cope with bullying. Big Will stopped making left turns and turned right.

Chapter 9 - **Why Me?**

Why me, was the question I asked myself for many years. I was born in the year 1968. This, I learned, was one of the worst years ever for blacks. We lost leaders like Martin Luther King Jr., Robert Kennedy, and many more. There were riots and fires, blacks was being beaten, washed away with water, locked up, and assaulted.

For years I questioned why I made it. For years, it was a joke of how small I was when I was born. I was told that I was born months early. I was a premature baby. It wasn't until I was grown that I learned that I wasn't expected to live. I also learned a secret that everyone knew but me. I learned from an argument with my little sister that my dad had beaten my mom so badly that neither of us was supposed to have made it. The doctor had to do emergency surgery to save me.

Today I feel that my being born was the cause of my mom and dad taking left turns. For many years I wished I would not have made it.

I was just a kid who was living a great life, so I thought, until my parents divorced. We ended up moving from a nice, middle class neighborhood to the Robert Taylor Homes, a public housing project on the south side of Chicago. I wondered if I did not want to remember how bad my dad use to beat my mom. See, I never blamed my dad, but hated my mom for leaving my dad. In all honesty, I really loved my mom and always wanted to be around her. When we came home from school one day and found that she was gone, I cried. I was told that she had left us and wasn't coming back.

For some reason I didn't believe it, and day after day I would come home looking for my mom. We lived in a very big house so I would try to remember which rooms I hadn't check the day before. I would run to the closet, and then jump down on the floor looking under the beds, thinking, "I got you." But never found her. We used to play hide-go-seek, and I knew she didn't leave me. I knew that if I keep looking I would find her. But I never did. I was starting to get mad at everyone in my family, because they didn't even seem to care anymore. I started thinking that they were all playing a joke on me, but it wasn't funny anymore.

My mom was gone, and everyone knew it, everyone but me. I couldn't see her leaving me. When my dad said to let it go, he stated that she was gone and was never coming back. Those words tore me apart.

***

I thought about the time when I got my little brother dressed. I believe my mom and dad were fighting, but I was rushing him to get dressed. We put on some of our mom's and dad's clothes in a hurry to get out of there. I'm not sure if I didn't want to remember the fights, but I did know that I wanted out of that house and needed to take my little brother with me.

We ran and ran, not knowing where we were going. I realized now that we were lost. I didn't tell my brother. I saw a park and took him to it. We were supposed to have been in school but instead were sitting on a bench in the park. Next thing we knew, the police drove up on us. We couldn't have been any more than six and seven years old. I was so happy to see the two officers. They took us to the ice cream truck, and we got to pick whatever we wanted. We were so happy, until we turned the corner and pulled up in front of our house. We were looking at each other. My brother and I started crying asking the officers if we could stay with them. The closer we got to the door, the more we cried. We begged and pleaded with these officers to not make us stay. We knew that we were going to get a beating from our dad for running away.

***

I wondered if this was the reason I grew up abusing women in my life. I also realized that this could be the reason I was so afraid of girlfriends in my life abandoning me.

My mom did come back with a guy who lived across the street from us. I wondered if this could be the reason I was jealous in every relationship I ever had. I ended up loving my stepdad but think that the damage had been done.

***

My whole life was full of left turns after that. I was one of few that made it through a lifestyle of left turns. I watched a lot of people die making left turns. I didn't know how I survived or why I suffered for so many years.

I'm writing these stories hoping to stop you from going down that same road of left turns. Most people didn't make it. I hope to at least make you think about it before making your next left turn, because it could be your last.

***

I found myself calling on God a lot in life, but only when I was in certain situations where I needed Him. I started feeling like I was using God, like when we moved into the projects. The first thing I said was, "God please help me make it through this one."

***

Years later when I was selling weed, I went to make a delivery when four guys came into the hall and pulled out guns. I knew when the woman didn't open her door for me, that I had been set up. They told me to put the weed, money, watch and everything else on the steps. I was no fool, I didn't want to give them anything, but with a gun at my head, I wasn't going to resist. Next thing I knew, the guy with the gun pulled the trigger at my head. When he did that something in me clicked. I grabbed the hand his gun was in and prayed. I called on God again, as his buddies beat me in the ribs. I tried running the guy backwards through the door, and then pulled him backwards, running my back into the door of the woman who had set me up. I was not letting go of that gun.

I got hit hard in the side and lost my grip on the gun. He took a few steps back and tried to fire it again but it didn't go off. He hit it hoping to make it fire. I forced myself up and ran back to him, hoping to get to him before the gun fired. I grabbed him and we struggled, again, bumping into the walls and people's doors. His buddies left him there fighting with me. As I ran backwards at the woman's door again, it opened, and I let the guy's hand go. He ran out into the hallway. I was breathing very hard, as I quickly grabbed my things off the steps. I pushed the woman into her apartment and locked the door. I had my fist balled up ready to knock her out but didn't.

I looked out her window at my car, not knowing if they were still out there or not. I closed my eyes for a couple seconds and said, "God please help me out of this one." I unlocked her door and walked fast to my car and drove away. All I could think of was how I had just escape death, again.

***

I watched a show about head injuries and learned that a single blow to your head can do very bad damage to someone for life. At worst, it could kill you. At that moment I stated, "Please don't let this be my problem." Because I remembered being hit in the head with a baseball bat, I was also stabbed a couple times in the head. I remembered the scuffle I had with a few policemen that turned ugly and resulted in me being kicked in the head with their steel toed shoes.

Or the time when I was fighting the police, I made them so mad that they hog tied me, my hands and feet were tied together. They threw me into the back of their car. A cop had just been killed days ago, and I said something I should not have said to them about the dead officer. They took me out and threw me head first onto the sidewalk. I could do nothing but call on God, hoping he heard me.

As I was beaten by officers, suffered in jail, placed into solitary confinement, and locked in a cell for 23 hours a day, guess who I called on?

***

I tried to sell crack but ended up a crack head, smoking crack hoping my heart wouldn't burst. I remember being so strung out on meth I couldn't think straight. I remember being kidnapped, beaten and left for dead. I remember running while people were shooting at me, hoping not to get one in my back, as I ran praying to God.

I would pray the prayer that I had prayed many times before as I was so drunk, throwing up saying things like, "God please save me, and I will never drink again."

When I sat in that courtroom hearing them talk about giving me 25 years to life. Guess who I called on? And the list goes on and on. I wondered why God saved my life so many times, when I was one of the worst kids, at times, just using Him when I needed Him.

At times, I questioned if I even believed in a God. One thing I do know is that He believed in me from the beginning, and that whenever I called on Him, He was there.

I sat in prison, in solitary confinement again, sad and hurting. I felt the presence of God so strong, it was as if my God came and sat right on my bed with me. We talked a lot; God became my best friend and has been walking with me ever since. I asked Him to change my life, and instantly I could feel something going on inside me.

I knew that once I walked out of prison, the real test would begin. He made it so I didn't go back to where I had lived, and before I knew it, my whole life had changed in ways I had no power over.

My big question to God, as the tears ran down my face was, "Why me?" I watched my friends die and went to many funerals. Knowing all the wrong I was doing, I couldn't help but ask again, "WHY ME LORD?"

I believe God gave me my answer. I was told to do all I could to help the next young man and or woman not go through this life the way I did. He told me that He let me live this terrible life to share it with you, and that my life just may save your life. I smiled and laid down for a good night sleep. My life has never been the same. He became my best friend, and I hope and pray to never turn my back on Him again.

Before you make that next left turn in your life, stop for a moment and ask yourself, "Could this be my final left turn in life? Could this turn send me to jail or prison? Could this turn take my life?" Figure out a way to start taking rights, and start living life, before it's too late.

The problem of drugs, guns, murder, domestic violence, gangs, rape, child abuse and so much more is not a Black, White, Hispanic, or any other racial problem.

No, it's not a Republican and Democrat problem. Our world needs to wake up now or never. Our kids are our future, and if we don't get this right, how can they?

I found my higher power, and I hope you will find yours. It took me years and a lot of tears. I went through a lot of hurt and pain. I even tried suicide, but He wouldn't let me go. He stopped guns from going off, on two occasions, at close range at my head.

I needed something and/or someone more powerful than I to have made it.

Look into yourself and try to figure out what it is you may need. People call on their higher power, some call on other things. All I want from you is to tap into something soon. If you're living wrong or feel like you have nowhere to turn or no one to turn to, please try something greater than yourself.

Just start taking right turns in life before a left turn takes your life. Try God. I feel like I lived most my life doing wrong for Satan. Why not try something else, something positive?

There was a time when I didn't even believe in God. Today I realize that if it wasn't for God, I would not have been here to write this for you. I'm not trying to push my God onto you, but I do know that if I can make it through it all and become a good man in our society today, you can too. No matter where you're at in life right now, you can change your outcome. Start today. If you don't know where to start, I would say start by taking right turns, and see how you like it.

Today I love the life I live. For years I prayed and talked to my God, not knowing what I was doing, or if there was even a God. I didn't know if He heard me or not. But as I look back over my life, I know He was there from the day I was born.

If God could be there for one of the worst kids ever, He will be there for you.

Bottom line, stop taking that left. Try right...

Endnote

WHAT WILL YOU DO?

If you think back to the stories, can you see the many left turns that were taken? Who made these turns? And could they have done things differently? (Explain)

Can you put yourself in any of the stories and tell someone what you would have done differently? (Explain)

Do you think you have it in you to **try** taking rights? I love life now more than ever and will never go back to that life of lefts.

I'm not trying to push my God on to you, but please believe me when I tell you He has never let me down the many times I faced death. He never once lied to me. Once upon a time I had very little belief in God, mainly when I was living a life of hell. Today I know why He let my life go the way it went and kept saving me over and over.

God said that He would turn evil to good. That's exactly what He did with my life.

He allowed me to live that evil life of hell so that I would share it with you for the good. From birth, this was His plan for me, I just never knew it until now. As I was growing up, I saw so much talent in kids that never made it. Don't let that kid be you. He put this passion in my heart to do my part in trying to help save lives. Could that life be yours?

My God made changes in my life that I could have never done myself. I used to live to do wrong; it was the only thing I knew. Are you in that place right now? There are ways out. Try right before it's too late. Left turns lead to hospitals, prisons, and **DEATH**. No matter where you're at in life right now, it's not too late. Let's put the guns down, no one wins, everyone loses. It's out of control when teachers have to have bullet proof shields just to do their jobs. This is not a race problem, it's a world problem. Do your part, think about this:

WILL THIS LEFT TURN I'M ABOUT TO TAKE BE MY LAST ONE WAY?

Reflections:

_____

_____

_____

_____

_____

_____

_____

_____

_____

_____

_____

_____

_____

_____

_____

_____

Reflections:

_____

_____

_____

_____

_____

_____

_____

_____

_____

_____

_____

_____

_____

_____

_____

_____

Other Books by Heart Thoughts Publishing

Intensive Faith Therapy – Vanessa Collins

The Promises of Jesus – Vanessa Collins

The Promises of God – Vanessa Collins

Transcending Greatness – Lawrence Perkins

Lil Fella's Big Dream – Lawrence Perkins

Upcoming Releases

A Healing Conversation – Edgar Gosa

Breakfast with God –Rev. Paul L. Jakes Jr.

Vision of an Outspoken Soul – LaKeishia Campbell

Scrambling to Breathe – Marcus McGhee

Visit us at **www.HeartThoughtsPublishing.com**

Or email us at

Info@HeartThoughtsPublishing.com

Made in the USA
Columbia, SC
10 February 2020